The Birthday Wish

Adapted by Mary Man-Kong
Based on the story by Devra Speregen
Illustrated by Federica Salfo, Francesco Legramandi, and Charles Pickens

A Random House PICTUREBACK® Book

Random House 🏠 New York

BARBIE and associated trademarks and trade dress are owned by, and used under license from, Mattel.
Copyright © 2017 Mattel. All Rights Reserved.
www.barbie.com
Published in the United States by Random House Children's Books, a division of Penguin Random House LLC, 1745 Broadway, New York, NY 10019, and in
Canada by Penguin Random House Canada Limited, Toronto. No part of this book may be reproduced or copied in any form without written permission
from the copyright owner. Pictureback, Random House, and the Random House colophon are registered trademarks of Penguin Random House LLC.
ISBN 978-1-5247-1646-2
randomhousekids.com   Printed in the United States of America   10 9 8 7 6 5 4

The day before her birthday party, Chelsea was playing catch in the backyard with her best friends, Jace and Zoie.

"I can't wait for your party tomorrow, Chelsea!" Zoie said. Then she gasped and covered her mouth. "Oops, sorry, Jace! I forgot you can't go!"

Jace had to visit his cousins in another town when Chelsea's party was taking place.

"It's okay," Jace said. "What are you going to wish for when you blow out your candles, Chelsea?"

Chelsea hadn't given her birthday wish much thought.

"You should wish for all the toys in the world!" her annoying neighbor, Otto, said as he tossed their ball to them.

"That's silly!" Chelsea said. "How would I even play with that many toys?"

"If you think birthday wishes are silly, I can always blow out your candles for you," Otto told her. "Then *I* could wish for all the toys in the world!"

That night, Chelsea thought about what Otto had said. What if Otto blew out her candles and ruined her birthday wish? She needed her wish ready for cake time tomorrow!

Chelsea yawned, then closed her eyes and drifted off to sleep.

Chelsea dreamed of flying a magical boat to Wispy Forest, where your hair transformed to show what you were thinking.

Chelsea was happy to see Barbie the Forest Princess and Locksley the Hare.

"Did you come to Wispy Forest to celebrate your birthday?" asked Barbie.

"Actually, I came here because I need help," Chelsea replied. "I don't know what to wish for when I blow out my candles."

"We can help you with that," said Locksley. "Do you want to be a Royal Princess?"

Chelsea thought about being a real princess, and magically, her hair began to transform into a crown! But just as quickly, it changed and stood straight up on her head!

Beneath a Golden Locks tree, someone was laughing. It was the Notto Prince!

"Notto!" Chelsea cried. Notto had put a friendly, hairy creature called a Mople on her head. Now it was standing up!

"Notto, I wish you would just leave me alone!" Chelsea exclaimed.

Hearing this, Locksley quickly hopped over to Notto's jet pack and pushed a button that sent him sailing into the sky.

"Birthday wish granted!" Locksley declared.

"Oh no!" Chelsea said. "When I said 'wish,' I didn't mean that was my birthday wish."

Barbie told Chelsea to follow Notto to Rainbow Cove to fix her mistake.

"Hi, Chelsea," said Barbie the Rainbow Queen. "Why do you look so worried on the day before your birthday?"

Chelsea told her how Locksley thought she had used her wish to send the Notto Prince away.

"Now I wish I'd never wished that wish," Chelsea said.

"You wish you'd never wished that wish?" Barbie repeated.

"Yeah, I feel bad!" said Chelsea.

"Well, that sounds simple enough," Barbie said as she waved her arms. Suddenly, a magic rainbow sailed around them and deposited the Notto Prince beside them!

"Hey, how'd I get here?" Notto asked in confusion.

The Junior Rainbow Princesses giggled and told him that Chelsea had wished for him to go away, but then she wished she'd never wished that wish.

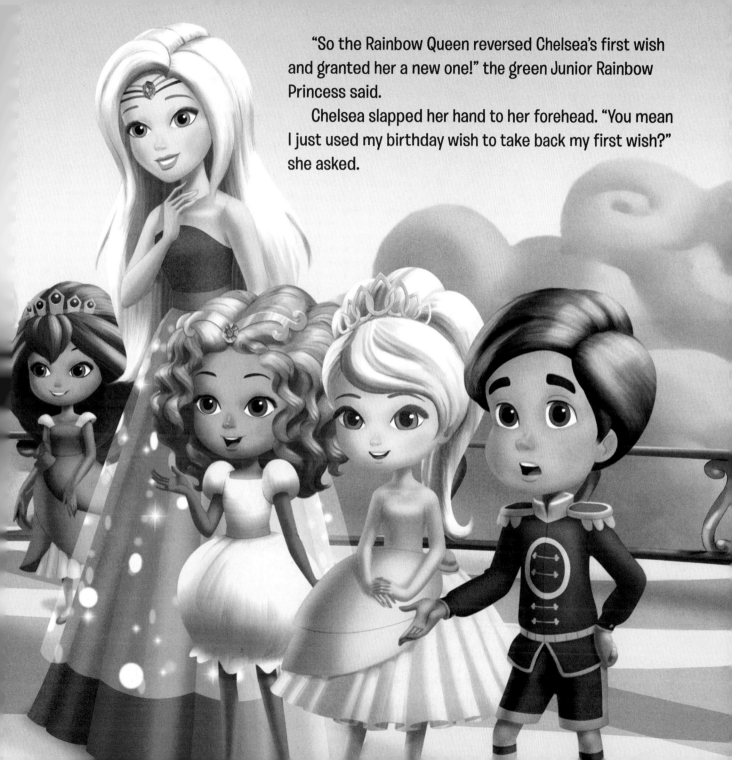

"So the Rainbow Queen reversed Chelsea's first wish and granted her a new one!" the green Junior Rainbow Princess said.

Chelsea slapped her hand to her forehead. "You mean I just used my birthday wish to take back my first wish?" she asked.

"So that's not what you wished for?" Barbie asked.

"I didn't mean for it to be my *birthday* wish," Chelsea explained.

"I think I know how to fix it," Barbie announced. "What you need is another birthday wish!"

All of a sudden, a beautiful birthday cake appeared!

Before Chelsea could make a wish, the Notto Prince stepped up to the cake and took a deep breath.

Chelsea gasped. "Notto, no!" she cried. But Notto wasn't listening. Chelsea closed her eyes and shouted: "I wish Notto wouldn't blow out my candle!"

Just then, a rainbow carried the prince high into the clouds. "I was just joking!" he shouted.

Chelsea watched in disbelief as Notto sailed farther from Rainbow Cove. "Looks like he's headed for Sweetville," Barbie said. "Maybe you can go after him and explain."

In Sweetville, Chelsea told Barbie the Sugar Spun Fairy how she'd accidentally wished for the Notto Prince to go away—twice! She felt bad and was trying to find him.

"Why don't you come with me to take this sleepy Strawberry Bear home," Barbie suggested. "We can look for the Notto Prince along the way."

As they walked, Barbie asked Chelsea what she really wanted for her birthday wish.

Chelsea already had great sisters, an adorable puppy, and fabulous best friends: Zoie and Jace.

Then Chelsea remembered Jace wasn't going to be at her birthday party.

"What I really want most is to celebrate my birthday with all my friends," she told Barbie.

As they reached the Strawberry Bear's house, Chelsea was surprised to find Notto waiting outside.

"I'm sorry for teasing you about blowing out your candle," Notto said.

"I'm sorry, too," Chelsea said. "For making you go away–twice!"

"It's okay," the Notto Prince said.

Inside the house, Chelsea saw everyone from Sweetville.
"Surprise!" they exclaimed.
The Marshmallow Pals, the Chocolate Bunnies, the Watermelon
Creature, and the other Strawberry Bears were all there.
"Happy birthday, Chelsea!" they cheered.

"We hope you like your surprise party," Barbie said.

"Want some help blowing out the candle?" the Notto Prince joked.

Chelsea laughed. "Sure!"

"Make a wish!" Barbie said.

Chelsea closed her eyes. She knew exactly what she was going to wish for.

The next thing Chelsea knew, she was in her bed back home. Her puppy, Honey, was licking her nose, trying to wake her up.

Chelsea heard her sister Barbie's voice in the backyard, and that was when it hit her: today was her birthday! She leaped out of bed and raced downstairs.

Chelsea burst through the back door and into the yard.
"Wow! This looks amazing!"
Barbie gave her sister a big hug. "Happy birthday, Chelsea!"
she said.

Chelsea had fun, and when it came time for her to make her birthday wish, Jace came running into her backyard! "I got home early!" he said. "I couldn't miss my best friend's birthday!"

"Yay!" Chelsea cheered.

She asked everyone to help her make a birthday wish and blow out the candle–but Chelsea's wish had already come true: *all* her friends were there to celebrate!